jF
TOL
Tolstoy, Leo, graf,
1828-1910.   98

The lion and the
puppy and other
stories for
children

$15.45

DATE		

THE LION AND THE PUPPY

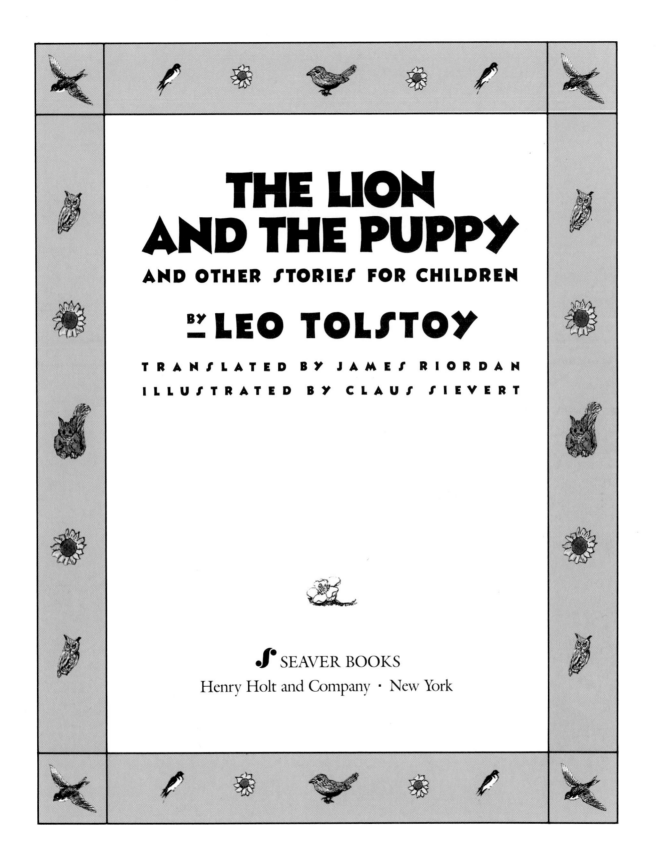

THE LION AND THE PUPPY

AND OTHER STORIES FOR CHILDREN

BY LEO TOLSTOY

TRANSLATED BY JAMES RIORDAN
ILLUSTRATED BY CLAUS SIEVERT

𝄑 SEAVER BOOKS

Henry Holt and Company · New York

Translation copyright © 1988 by James Riordan
Illustrations copyright © 1988 by Claus Sievert
All rights reserved, including the right to reproduce this
book or portions thereof in any form.
Published by Seaver Books/Henry Holt and Company, Inc.,
115 West 18th Street, New York, New York 10011.
Published in Canada by Fitzhenry & Whiteside Limited,
195 Allstate Parkway, Markham, Ontario L3R 4T8.

Library of Congress Cataloging-in-Publication Data
Tolstoy, Leo, graf, 1828–1910.
The lion and the puppy.
1. Tolstoy, Leo, graf, 1828–1910—Translations,
English.   2. Short stories, Russian—Translations
into English.   I. Sievert, Claus.   II. Title.
PG3366.A13R56   1988   891.73′3   87-28653
ISBN 0-8050-0735-0

First Edition

Printed in Singapore
1 3 5 7 9 10 8 6 4 2

ISBN 0-8050-0735-0

CONTENTS

Introduction   vii

Translator's Note   xi

The Lion and the Puppy   1

Little Cottontop   3

Escape of a Dancing Bear   6

Masha and the Mushrooms   10

Death of a Bird-Cherry Tree   12

Little Philip Who Wanted to Go to School   15

A Young Boy's Story of How a Storm Caught
Him in the Forest   18

The King and the Shirt   19

Two Brothers Learn a Lesson   22

A Young Boy's Story of How He Found Queen Bees
for His Granddad   25

The Tired Swan   27

The Old Fire-Dog   31

Two Merchants   32

The Old Poplar   35

How Many Geese Make Six?   38

The "Dead" Man and the Bear   40

The Little Bird   42

The Plum Stone   45

Better to Be Lean and Free than Plump and Chained   47

A Young Boy's Story of How He Did Not Go to Town   50

Dew upon the Grass   52

Uncle Jacob's Dog   54

Why Wolves Are Mean and Squirrels Frisky   56

The Ants   58

From an Acorn Grew an Oak Tree Tall   60

INTRODUCTION:
LEO TOLSTOY — STORIES FOR CHILDREN

Do you know the story of the Selfish Giant who was never visited by Spring until he opened up his garden to children? Here is a true story about a Russian nobleman who not only let children into the garden of his great country home, he also taught them to read and write. He even wrote the stories in this book for them.

And well he might. For he was one of the greatest storytellers that ever lived, a giant among authors.

His name was Leo Tolstoy.

This is how he came to write his stories for children.

Many years ago, in Russia, behind a big stone wall, there was a beautiful garden with soft green grass and glades of silver birch. The village children were not allowed into this garden. All they could see as they peered through the tall iron railings of the gate was a distant lake shimmering through the trees beyond a neatly swept drive of stately poplars. And somewhere in the grounds of that great garden, they knew, there stood a big house in which a famous gentleman lived.

The notice on the gates said "Yasnaya Polyana," which in Russian means "Clear Glades."

CLEAR GLADES
Country House of Count L. N. Tolstoy

That was plain enough. The children knew they had to keep out.

How surprised—and not a little afraid—they were when one day they heard that the Count had summoned them to his mansion. The word soon spread through the village. What did he want them for? Rumor had it that he wanted to teach them to read and write.

What a strange idea!

In those days there were few enough schools in the towns, fewer still in the countryside. Very, very rarely could a villager read or write. If a letter needed to be written, people went to the deacon and had to pay a tidy sum for it. There were no books in the village, no newspapers, no schools.

Yet now it seemed that the Count had a mind to open a school for poor children. And to teach them himself.

The children were shy. But on the appointed day they put on their Sunday best—a clean shirt and fresh birch-bark shoes—smoothed down their unkempt hair with yellow sunflower oil or brown rye juice, and set off in a crowd for the Big House.

The year was 1849. The gold and russet trees of autumn had laid a crisp carpet of leaves along the drive, as the children made their way to the house. Once past the dark, still waters of the lake, a big house suddenly came into view, set back behind the trees. The tall two-story building seemed like a palace to boys and girls who had grown up in squat smoke-begrimed huts under straw-thatched roofs. Nervously, the knots of village children stood before the house, waiting for the Count to appear.

Finally he appeared on the veranda—a tall, broad-shouldered figure with long straggly hair, a large fleshy nose, and a bushy black beard. As he fixed them with his fierce stare, from under the most enormous eyebrows, the children drew back in alarm. Yet the moment he smiled and spoke, their shyness seemed to melt away.

The school at Clear Glades was open all day long, and children could come and go as they pleased. No one forced them to attend, and no one forced any lessons upon them. Each child did whatever took her or his fancy—drawing, reading, writing, sports. And, by all accounts, the children came to the school very willingly, some arriving as early as seven in the morning and staying until late evening. Such was their eagerness to learn.

But it was not all sitting at desks. Tolstoy loved games. In summer he taught the children croquet on his lawn, and rigged up a small gym in the barn. He took them on nature rambles through the woods and down to the river to swim. And when the winter snows and ice came, there was no end to the games the children played: speeding downhill on great sleds, snowballing, tumbling in the snow—with the Count himself in the thick of them! They cleared the snow from the big lake to make a skating rink; they held races there, but few could beat Tolstoy, who was an excellent skater.

At Christmastime he decorated a big fir tree inside his house and held a party for all the children on his estate. Of course, the thin ragged village children had never had such a party in their lives.

In those days children's lives were hard. As soon as they were strong enough—about the age of ten—they had to drive a wooden plow and toil in the fields from dawn to dusk. Childhood ended early in Russia at that time; peasant families were but serfs, slaves to the lords.

Yet here was a lord, Count Tolstoy, who was opening the doors of his house, with its polished wooden floors, lofty ceilings, and bright windows, to the village children. It all seemed a fairy tale.

But it was real enough. And so was their teacher's love for them. Throughout his long life Tolstoy loved children. It hurt him to see so much poverty and ignorance among the children in the countryside. But he also knew how miserable the lives of the children in the towns were. His heart ached at the sound of the factory whistles at dawn and dusk from the mill beyond the village. He once visited that mill and wrote in his diary:

I visited a stocking mill and learned what the whistles mean. At five o'clock in the morning a boy takes his stand beside a machine and stays there till eight. At eight he drinks tea and then stands till midday; and at one he begins again and stands till four; then he works through from half past four to eight in the evening. Every day, seven days a week. That's what the whistles mean we hear in our beds.

He wondered how such children had time to live, children whom whistles set in motion at five in the morning and stopped at eight in the evening. When would they learn, read books, have time to play?

Tolstoy's school was the first in Russia for village children. But when he came to seek school books that were easy to read and interesting he was disappointed. What few children's books existed were dull and more likely to put out the spark of interest than kindle it.

So the great writer, known throughout the world for his famous books, sat down to write stories for children that were easy to read and interesting, that would teach right from wrong, good from bad. Even though his great works took up much of his time and energy, he always found time for the children.

The stories he wrote were not only for the village children around Clear Glades. They were intended for all girls and boys who wish to open up their hearts to truth and beauty.

TRANSLATOR'S NOTE

The stories are taken from Tolstoy's *Azbuka* (Primer) which consisted of four "Russian Reading Books," four "Slav Reading Books," a section on teaching reading, handwriting, and arithmetic, and guidance for teachers. Although the Primer was not published until 1872, it was based on notebooks Tolstoy had kept from his first teaching experience at his school for peasant children at Yasnaya Polyana (Clear Glades) from 1849 and at other schools he founded for peasant children in the Tula Province.

The stories vary widely: some are based on Aesop's fables, others on Russian and foreign folk tales, some on nature studies, and others on the work of children themselves. As an example of the latter, the "Young Boy's Stories" all come from the storytelling of peasant children whom Tolstoy encouraged to read and write "in their own words."

What distinguishes all the stories in the Primer from children's stories current in Russian schools at that time is that they are largely free from the heavy moralistic homilies and religious preaching that Tolstoy abhorred. Moreover, they are written in a simple language style "for a new audience," as Tolstoy put it, "that has to be counted in many thousands, even millions."

The present versions are taken from *Novaya azbuka* (New Primer) and the four *Russkie knigi dlya chteniya* (Russian Reading Books) edited by Tolstoy for the 1875 edition. They are contained in L. N. Tolstoy, *Sobranie sochineniy v 14 tomkakh*, tom desyaty (*Collected Works in 14 Volumes*, vol. 10), Moscow, 1952.

THE LION AND THE PUPPY

THE LION AND THE PUPPY

There was once a zoo in London that took stray cats and dogs to feed its wild animals. One time, a visitor to the zoo picked up a puppy from the street and took it along with him. Handing it over at the gate, he watched the keeper throw the hapless puppy into the lion's cage.

Poor little dog.

Tail between its legs, it squeezed itself into the corner of the cage as the lion came closer and closer.

Suddenly, the lion stopped and began to sniff his victim. Tickled by the lion's whiskers, the puppy rolled over and wagged its tail playfully. At that, the lion prodded it uncertainly with his paw, pushing it to and fro over the floor of his cage.

To the lion's surprise, the little dog nimbly jumped up and stood on its hind legs, begging.

Puzzled, the lion stared at the dog, shifting his massive head slowly from side to side, not knowing what to make of this funny little animal.

But he let it be.

At feeding time, when the keeper tossed meat into the cage, the lion tore off a piece for the puppy. And at sunset, as the lion lay down to sleep, the puppy lay alongside him, resting its tiny head on the lion's great paws.

1

From that day on the lion and the puppy lived together in the same cage: the lion sharing his food, never harming his companion, sleeping alongside and, now and then, playing with it.

Then, one day, a fine gentleman visited the zoo and straightaway recognized his long-lost pet. The keeper was informed and, of course, would willingly have handed it over had not the lion raged and roared every time he approached the puppy. In the end he gave up and the gentleman had to go home empty-handed.

So the lion and the puppy stayed together; thus it continued for a whole year, until one day the little dog fell sick. And in a short space of time it died.

What a change came over the lion! All the while he licked and sniffed his friend, prodding it with his paw. At last, realizing it was indeed dead, the lion sprang up, his mane quivering with rage. He stalked about the cage, swinging his tail fiercely. He flung himself against the iron bars and tore at the wooden floorboards.

All day long he roared in his anguish until finally he sank down beside his dead companion. And he was quiet.

But when the keeper tried to remove the dead puppy, the lion growled menacingly and would not let him near. After a while, the keeper had an idea. Thinking a new puppy would make the lion forget his grief, he thrust another dog between the bars.

But the lion ignored the puppy.

Then, gently, he put his paws about his cold little friend and lay grieving for a full five days.

And on the sixth day the lion died.

LITTLE COTTONTOP

There was once an old man and old woman. One day the old man went off to the fields to plow, while the old woman stayed home to make pancakes. When the pancakes were ready, she said to herself:

"If only we had a son to take some pancakes to his father."

All of a sudden, a little boy popped out of a pile of cotton, piping, "Hello there, Mummy!"

What a fright he gave the old woman.

"Where did you spring from, Sonny? What's your name?"

Said the lad in reply, "You spun some cotton, Mummy, and left it in the frame. That's where I hatched out. My name is Little Cottontop. Now give me the pancakes and I'll take them to Daddy."

Once more she was surprised.

"*You* will take them, Cottontop?"

"Sure I will."

So the old woman wrapped the pancakes into a bundle and gave them to the little boy. Little Cottontop took the bundle and ran with it over his shoulder to the fields.

As he crossed the field he found his way barred by a clod of earth.

"Daddy, Daddy," he called. "Help me over the clod of earth! I've brought you some pancakes."

The old man could hear someone calling him, and as he went toward the sound he suddenly saw the little fellow, no bigger than a clod of earth.

"Where did you spring from, Sonny?" he asked.

"I hatched out of a pile of cotton, Daddy," he said, handing him the pancakes.

As he sat down to eat, he heard the boy call, "Hey, Daddy, can I try plowing?"

The old man shook his head. "You won't have the strength," he said.

But Little Cottontop took hold of the plow and began to till the field, singing as he went.

Meantime, a wealthy gentleman was passing by and saw the old man sitting at his meal, with his horse plowing on its own. So the gentleman stepped down from his carriage and called to the old man:

"How do you get your horse to plow by itself?"

"That's my son plowing," answered the old man. "That's him singing, too."

At that the gentleman came closer, heard the singing, and caught a glimpse of Little Cottontop.

"Good gracious," he exclaimed. "Sell that lad to me, old fellow."

But the old man shook his head. "No, I cannot, he's all I have."

But Cottontop whispered in his ear, "Go on, Daddy, I'll run away from him."

So the poor peasant sold the boy for a hundred rubles. The gentleman handed over the money, took the lad, wrapped him in a handkerchief, and put him into his pocket. When he arrived home he said to his wife:

"I've a big surprise for you, my dear."

"Oh, do show it to me," she said in delight.

The gentleman pulled the handkerchief from his pocket and unwrapped it, but there was nothing there. Little Cottontop had run back to his father.

ESCAPE OF
A DANCING BEAR

When I was a boy some men hereabouts used to catch bear cubs and teach them to dance. Then, when they grew older, the bears were dressed up and taken round the fairs. It was the custom for one person to lead the bear, while the other would dress up as a goat and beat a drum.

One such party was once on its way to a fair at Novgorod, a young boy in goatskin leading the way and banging a drum. As was usual for the Novgorod spring fair, the town was packed with visitors from all over Russia and the dancing bear drew much attention, earning his master a tidy sum of money.

At the end of the day, the master, the boy, and the dancing bear made their way to an inn where they gave a last show in the yard. This time they received plenty of wine in reward. The master gratefully gulped down his wine, giving some to the boy and a whole dishful to Old Bruno the Bear.

At nightfall, the party had to spend the night in a field beyond the town. The master tied the bear's chain around his own waist, as he stretched out on the ground to sleep. Being somewhat tired and tipsy, he was soon snoring contentedly; so, too, was the boy, his assistant. Thus the two slumbered on soundly until daybreak.

When the master awoke, he found to his alarm that the bear was missing. Rousing his assistant, he rushed off in search of the runaway bear. The grass being high, they could plainly see the bear's tracks leading into the forest. They realized that it would be almost impossible to catch the bear once he reached the shelter of the woods.

The boy was all for giving up the chase, but the old man was stubborn.

"That bear's our living, lad," he said. "It took five years to train him. If we don't find him we're dead broke—worse than beggars. No, I'll find that brown villain yet!"

On they went into the trees until, toward dusk, they came to a broad meadow. Just as they sank down to rest, the sounds of a chain clanking nearby brought them quickly to their feet; and they stole cautiously toward the noise.

There in a clearing was the bear: the poor old fellow was shuffling along, pulling the chain and, with his paws, trying to tear the wicked muzzle from his snout. As soon as he spotted his old master, he gave a fearful roar and bared his yellow teeth. The boy was frightened and would have fled had not his master pulled him after the bear.

Old Bruno bellowed even more fearfully and lumbered off into the trees. Clearly, it was foolhardy to pursue him into the depths of the forest where they might encounter more bears or even wolves. But the master had an idea.

"Put on the goat's mask and bang your drum," he told the boy.

At the same time he shouted gruffly to the bear, just as he did when he was showing him off, "Dance, Bruno, dance!"

All of a sudden the bear stopped in his tracks, stood up on his hind legs, and began to twirl around slowly. In the meantime, his wily master crept closer, shouting and calling, "Dance, Bruno, dance!"

His assistant all the while clowned before the bear, beating the drum and singing. When the master was quite near, he lunged forward to grab

the chain. The bear saw the ruse too late, roared helplessly, and tried to escape. But the master clung on tightly.

And that was how Old Bruno came to be recaptured. Once again he was led round the fairs and inns, forever twirling, clowning, and dancing in his chains.

For people's amusement.

MASHA AND THE MUSHROOMS

Two little sisters were walking home from gathering mushrooms when they came to a railway track. Thinking no train was near, they climbed over a rail and were crossing the line when, from out of nowhere, a great locomotive whistled shrilly.

The two little girls were scared out of their wits. As the bigger girl held back, her little sister dashed forward to the middle of the track.

"Masha, Masha!" cried her sister. "Go on, go on. Cross the track quickly."

But the train made such a clattering as it approached that Masha did not hear; she thought she was being called back. And as she turned, the poor girl stumbled and fell, scattering the mushrooms from her basket all over the railway track.

In a panic, the girl tried quickly to gather them up.

The train was now quite near. Its driver hollered and pulled the whistle for all he was worth, and in the meantime Masha's sister was screaming frantically to her:

"Leave the mushrooms! Oh, let them be!"

Through the din, however, the little girl heard only "the mushrooms" and, thinking her sister had said to pick them up, she was crawling along the track on hands and knees, picking up her scattered mushrooms.

The train was now bearing down on her. . . . There was nothing anyone could do. And, with one despairing whistle, the great monster was upon her.

Masha's sister could not bear to look: she hid her head in her hands in horror. Ashen-faced, the train's passengers stared dumbly from the windows, while the guard peered back along the track to see what had become of the poor girl.

There she was, face pressed to the ground, lying motionless between the rails. And then, as the train rumbled on its way, she suddenly lifted her head, picked up the rest of her mushrooms, and ran off, unharmed, to her sister.

DEATH OF A BIRD-CHERRY TREE

A bird-cherry had grown wild beside the path to the nut grove and was blocking out the sunlight from our young hazel trees. For a long time I pondered over it: Should I or should I not cut down the tree?

It seemed a shame to kill such a beautiful thing.

The bird-cherry was more of a tree than a bush, some three feet in girth and twelve feet high, all gnarled and forked, and graced with a white sweet-scented blossom whose fragrance wafted even as far as the house.

I would surely have let it live had not one of my woodmen begun the job one morning. No doubt I had told him sometime earlier to grub out all the bird-cherry.

When I came on the scene his axe had already bitten a good foot out of the trunk; and the sap was squealing its complaint at each blow of the axe.

"Oh, well, perhaps it's all for the good," I sighed, taking up an axe and lending a hand.

With the chips flying about and the sweet smell of freshly hewn wood in my nostrils, all my doubts about the bird-cherry vanished. My mind was now set on felling the tree. And when we laid aside our axes

and put our shoulders to the tree, trying to push it over, I felt a sense of triumph course through my veins. We heaved hard: the leaves trembled, showering us with dewdrops and little white bouquets of petals.

And then an unnerving sound came from inside the very soul of that tree. It was as if someone was screaming in unbearable pain, a tearing, wrenching, long drawn-out scream.

Gripped by a mixture of fear and sorrow, we hastily gave a last heave and, with a heartrending, sobbing sigh, the tree shuddered and fell.

After the first crash, the branches and blossoms lay trembling for a while, then lay still. For several moments, the woodman and I stood silent, unable to speak. Then, in the awkward hush, my companion muttered:

"Whew, she don't die easy, Sir!"

A lump in my throat blocked my words, and I turned quickly to make my way back to the house. I did not dare glance back.

LITTLE PHILIP WHO WANTED TO GO TO SCHOOL

Philip was too young to go to school. But when, at the end of the summer holidays, the older children went off to school, Philip got ready to go too.

His mother was surprised.

"Where are you going, Philip?"

"To school."

"But you're still too young," she said with a smile.

His playmates were all in school. Father had gone off early that morning to work. And now mother had gone out shopping. So Philip was left at home alone—apart from Grannie, who was still asleep.

Before long he was bored all by himself. And with Grannie snoring softly in the next room, he crept into the hall, put on his coat and, not finding his own cap, picked up father's old fur hat, and set off through the snow to school.

The school stood beyond the village by the old church. To reach it Philip had to walk down the village street and up a hill. As he was walking past some cottages, however, the guard dogs—a terrier and a fierce Alsatian—began to snap at his heels. He began to run, then stumbled and fell. Just then an old man came out of a nearby cottage and drove off the dogs.

15

"Hey, young fellow-me-lad, what's your hurry?" he asked kindly.

But Philip gathered himself up and hurried off as best he could through the snow. In no time at all he arrived at the school and quickly dodged through the big doors. No one was to be seen in the hall, though he could hear voices from behind a door.

All of a sudden, doubt seized him: What would the teacher say? If he returned home, though, he risked being bitten by the dogs.

"Why aren't you in class?" snapped a gruff voice behind him.

It was the school janitor.

"In you go, shoo-shoo."

So little Philip opened the door of the classroom, taking off his father's hat as he went. The class was full of children, each chattering away, as a tall schoolmaster in a long red scarf paced up and down between the desks.

"What do you want, boy?" shouted the lanky fellow at Philip.

The lad stood silently in the doorway, looking down at his felt boots.

"Well, speak up, who are you?"

Philip kept silent.

"Have you no tongue, boy? Go back home if you cannot speak."

Philip wanted to speak so much. But the words stuck in his throat. He looked up at the teacher and burst into tears.

At that the man took pity on him and, putting his arm around Philip's shoulders, he turned to the class, asking if anyone knew him.

"He's Philip, Michael's brother," said a voice. "He can't wait to come to school, but his mother says he's too young."

"Ah-ha," exclaimed the teacher, stroking his beard. "Well, go and sit on the bench, alongside your brother. Later I'll have a talk with your mother about your coming to school."

When the teacher came to show Philip the alphabet, he was surprised to find the boy already knew it. He could even read a little.

"Let's see you spell your name, if you can," said the teacher with a smile.

16

"Fee-Fi-Lee-Li-Ip-Pi."

All the class laughed.

"Well done," said the teacher. "Who taught you to spell?"

Philip now grew bolder.

"Michael did. But I . . . I'm very quick at learning. . . . It didn't take me long."

The teacher laughed and said, "Not so fast, young man. You must learn to walk before you can run."

Philip's first day at school passed all too quickly.

And from then on he went to school every day.

A YOUNG BOY'S STORY OF HOW A STORM CAUGHT HIM IN THE FOREST

When I was little, Mother sent me for mushrooms in the woods. I reached the woods, gathered some mushrooms, and was just about to go home when all at once it turned dark, began to thunder, and rain came down. I was scared stiff and took shelter under a big oak tree. Such bright lightning flashed that it hurt my eyes and I had to screw them up. Above my head something began to creak and crack and I felt a sudden blow on the head. I fell forward and lay there until the rain stopped.

When I came to, the whole forest was dripping water, the birds were singing, and sunlight was dancing in the trees. The big oak had broken up and smoke was rising from the stump. All around me were pieces of oak. My smock was all wet and clinging to my body. I had a bump on my head and it ached a lot.

When I found my hat, I picked up the mushrooms and ran home. The house was deserted, so I took some bread from the table, climbed up on the stove, and fell asleep. When I awoke I could see that my mushrooms had already been fried and put on the table for tea.

I shouted down, "What are you eating without me for?"

And they said, "What are you sleeping for? Come and have your tea."

THE KING
AND THE SHIRT

Once a king fell gravely ill and gave an order that half his realm would go to whoever could cure him.

At that, all the wise men gathered to decide how to cure the king. Nobody knew. In the end, a wise man arrived to declare that the king could be cured on one condition.

"If a happy man can be found, the shirt taken from his back and put upon the king, the king will recover."

So the king sent messengers all over his kingdom to find a happy man, yet none could be found. There was not one man who was content with everything. Whoever was rich was ill; whoever was healthy was poor; whoever was healthy and rich had a mean wife or wicked children. Everyone complained about something.

Late one night the king's son was riding past a poor cottage when he heard someone say:

"Right, thank the Lord, I've done my stint, eaten my fill and can rest in peace. What else do I need?"

The prince was delighted to have found a happy man at last, and gave orders for the man's shirt to be taken to the king. He would, of course, pay the man as much money as he wished. But when the envoys entered the cottage to take the man's shirt, they found he was so poor he had no shirt upon his back at all.

TWO BROTHERS LEARN A LESSON

Two brothers had been walking since first dawn and, by noon, were tired and dusty, so they lay down to rest in a woodland glade.

On awakening they were surprised to find a stone before them, with an inscription faint and ancient. After much pondering, these were the words they read:

Whosoever finds this Stone
Should follow the Sunrise
Into the Forest Depths.
Within the Forest is a Stream
Which he must cross.
On the Far Bank will be a
Mother Bear with her Cubs.
He should take those Cubs
From their Mother and run
To a distant Hill
Without a backward Glance.
Upon that Hill stands a Castle,
And within that Castle
He will find Good Fortune.

For a time the brothers were silent, unable to make up their minds. Then the younger brother boldly exclaimed:

"Come on, Brother, let's go together. Should the fates be kind, we may swim the stream, take the cubs to the castle, and strike it rich."

But his brother reproached him.

"I certainly shall not go into the forest for bear cubs, and I advise you against it, too. How do we know the words are true? And even if they are and we enter the forest, night will fall before long and we'll lose our way. Even if we found the stream, how would we cross it? Even if we were to cross it, how would we take the cubs from their mother? And another thing: even if we were to take the cubs, we could hardly reach the hill without a rest. Nor does the Stone tell us what is the good fortune awaiting us at the castle. Perhaps we have no need of it!"

But the younger brother said:

"We've nothing to lose by trying. Anyway, if we don't try our luck, someone else may come along, find the Stone, and take the prize. If you really want something you've to work hard for it. Nothing ventured nothing gained."

"Be content with what you've got," said the other. "A bird in the hand is worth two in the bush."

There was no agreeing. So in the end, off went the younger man, leaving his brother behind.

He had not gone far into the forest when he came upon a stream, easily swam across it, and spied a mother bear asleep on the bank. Snatching up her cubs, he dashed off without a backward glance, toward a distant hill on whose crown stood a castle. As he ran up the hill, he was astonished to see the castle doors swing open and a great procession emerge, drawing a golden carriage. The people came toward him with great cheers, swept him up, deposited him upon the carriage's crimson cushions, and drove back to the castle to crown him King.

That was the prize of which the Stone had spoken!

The young man reigned a full five years, but in the sixth year misfortune befell him. Without warning, his castle was attacked by another king, even mightier than himself, and he was driven out.

He wandered alone back into the forest, swam across the same stream, and eventually arrived at his brother's cottage. The elder brother was now living a modest life in a modest way, neither well-to-do nor wanting for food.

How pleased the brothers were to meet again. Over a glass of this and a bowl of that, they recounted their adventures. And at the end of the telling, they each sat back contented.

Said the elder:

"Now you see the wisdom of my choice. All the while I've lived in peace and tranquillity; and though you've been king, you're now a pauper, worse off than before."

But the younger smiled.

"I have no regrets," he said. "I may be poor in worldly goods, but what wonderful memories I have to treasure!"

A YOUNG BOY'S STORY OF HOW HE FOUND QUEEN BEES FOR HIS GRANDDAD

My granddad used to spend his summers in a bee garden. When I visited him he would give me some honey.

Once, I had gone to the bee garden and was walking between the hives. I was not frightened of bees because Granddad had taught me to be quiet and still as I approached them. And the bees had grown used to me and did not sting me. But that day I heard something making an awful din in one of the hives. So I went to Granddad in his little hut and told him about it.

He came with me, listened carefully, and said:

"One swarm, the primer, has already left this hive with the old queen bee; and now young queen bees are hatching out. Tomorrow they'll fly off with other swarms."

I asked Granddad what sort of bees the queens were, and he said:

"Well, a queen bee is just like an emperor among the people. Without her there would be no bees."

"But what does she look like?" I asked.

"Come here tomorrow," he said, "and, God willing, they'll be swarming. I'll show you and give you some honey."

Next day when I visited Granddad he had two swarms of bees in

25

cardboard boxes on his porch. Granddad told me to put on a face net that covered my neck. Then he took one swarm of bees in a cardboard box and carried it to the bee garden. How the bees buzzed in their box! I was a bit scared of them and thrust my hands deep into my jacket pockets. But since I so wanted to take a look at the queen bee I followed Granddad.

Once in the garden, Granddad went up to an empty wooden trough, opened the cardboard box, and tipped the bees out of it into the trough. The bees crawled along the trough into a hollow log attached to it, trumpeting all the while, as Granddad poked them with his broom.

And there was the queen! He pointed her out with his broom.

She had a long body and short wings. At once she mingled with the others and soon was lost from sight.

Then Granddad took off my face net and led me back to the hut, where he gave me a big piece of honey. As I ate it I got it smeared all over my face and hands, so when I came home my mother said:

"Your silly old Granddad's been spoiling you with honey again!"

"But he gave me honey," I said, "for finding him a hive of young queen bees yesterday, and just now we've been planting a new swarm together."

THE TIRED SWAN

Across the open sea flew a flock of swans to warmer climes. Farther, yet farther they winged their way through golden dawns and crimson sunsets, cloudless days and stormy nights, on and on without a rest above the shifting waters.

Beating their graceful wings in tuneful rhythm like some angelic choir, the tired swans longed for repose, a haven to rest their aching bodies. But there was no stopping place on their perilous journey. Nothing but the boundless sky above and the forbidding sea below.

It was night. The moon cast a violet haze upon the water and lit up a lone white figure steadily falling behind the flying group. All of a sudden, with a resigned quiver of its tired wings, it ceased to flap and plunged down toward the ocean.

Meantime, its companions flew on without a backward glance, their bodies arched in graceful silhouette against the moonlit sky. No silent witness to the loss.

Sending up a sudden spray, the lone swan landed on the water; the sea bobbed and bounced beneath it as it floated on the angry waves.

By now the flock of swans was no more than a thin white line smeared across the distant sky. And in the still of night the lone swan

barely caught the faint swish of beating wings. Its sad gaze followed them out of sight until, with a heaving sigh, it curved back its neck and closed its tired eyes.

It made no struggle: the sea rose and fell with it into the wide rolling waves. And at dawn a light breeze ruffled its feathers and sprinkled glistening drops upon its pure white breast.

Its eyes opened. It stretched its neck, shook its wings as if reaching for the blushing dawn, and then tried to fly, its feet making a watery furrow along the surface of the sea.

And then, with a final thrust, it rose above the water.

Higher, ever higher, until at last it reached the open sky. And it flew on alone above the silvery waves.

THE OLD FIRE-DOG

Careless parents sometimes go out and leave their children at home alone. If a fire should break out the children could well die, for in their panic the little ones often keep silent and hide, and no one can find them through the smoke.

Special fire-dogs used to be trained to save children. When a house caught fire, the firemen would send in their dogs to bring out any little ones from the blazing building. One famous dog rescued as many as a dozen children. Here is the story of one of his rescues.

When firemen once arrived at a burning house, they were met by a sobbing woman who told them that her two-year-old daughter was still trapped in the blazing house. The famous fire-dog was sent in.

He dashed through the smoke into the building and up the stairs. Several minutes later he came running out of the door, holding the little girl by her nightgown.

The firemen patted the good old fire-dog, inspecting his fur to see that it had not been singed in the fire. But the brave dog strained back toward the house. Thinking there must be someone left in the building, the firemen let him go.

Bounding through the flames and smoke, the dog soon reappeared with another bundle in his teeth. The crowd gathered around in silence to take a closer look. Then smiles gradually spread over all the faces.

For the old fire-dog was carrying a big rag doll.

31

TWO MERCHANTS

A poor merchant once went on his travels, leaving all his iron merchandise with a rich merchant for safekeeping. When he returned, he went to the wealthy merchant and asked for his ironwares back.

But the wealthy merchant had already sold them and now had to make his excuses.

"I'm sorry to say that your iron is all gone."

"What happened?"

"It's like this: I stored your wares in my barn, and the mice came and ate them. They finished off the whole lot. I myself saw them nibbling at it. Go and see if you don't believe me."

The poor merchant did not bother to argue. He simply said:

"What is there to see? I believe you. I know mice are always eating iron."

And the poor merchant went off.

Once outside, he saw the rich merchant's son playing in the yard, and he persuaded the boy to come along with him.

Next day the wealthy merchant met the poor man and told him of his misfortune. His son had disappeared. Had he not seen or heard anything?

To which the poor merchant said, "Now that you ask, I did see something. I was just leaving your house yesterday when a hawk flew down and snatched up your son."

The wealthy merchant flew into a rage, crying, "How dare you make fun of me. Everybody knows hawks don't carry off children."

"But I'm not making fun of you," said the poor man. "Why should a hawk not carry off a boy, when mice can eat a hundred pounds of iron?"

At that the wealthy merchant understood.

"Mice did not eat your iron," he said. "I sold it and will pay you double."

"In that case, a hawk did not carry off your son," replied the other. "I'll bring him back at once."

THE OLD POPLAR

For five years our garden was neglected. Then I hired some workers with axes and spades and we went to work in the garden. We cut down and hewed out deadwood and brambles and the odd bush and tree. The poplar and bird-cherry were the worst culprits in being overgrown and stunting other trees. The poplar comes up from the roots, so you simply cannot cut it down, you have to grub out the roots.

Beyond the lake stood a huge poplar, two armfuls in girth. Around it was a glade all overgrown with poplar shoots. I gave the order to cut them down. I wanted the place to be lighter, neater, and most of all, I wanted to make life easier for the old poplar, for I thought all those young trees were coming from it and drawing the sap out of it.

As we were cutting down those young saplings, now and again I had a pang of conscience as we dug out their sap-rich roots. It took four of us to pull up one half-hewn sapling; it was hanging on to its life for all it was worth and did not want to die. And I thought to myself, "They evidently need to live if they cling on to life so firmly."

But we had to cut them down, so I did. Only subsequently, when it was too late, did I realize we should not have destroyed them.

I had thought that the shoots drew sap from the old poplar, but it

turned out to be the other way around. Once I had cut them down the old poplar began to die. When leaves began to appear I noticed that half its boughs were bare, and that summer it withered altogether. It had been dying for some time and, knowing its end was near, had transferred life to its shoots.

That is why they grew so quickly. In wanting to make life easier for it I had killed all its children.

HOW MANY GEESE MAKE SIX?

A poor peasant once went to the squire to ask for food. It did not seem proper to go empty-handed, so he stole a neighbor's goose, roasted it, tucked it under his arm, and took the bird with him to the manor.

Surprised and not a little suspicious, the squire accepted the roast goose but told the peasant:

"Thank you for the goose. But you give me a problem: You see, I have a wife, two sons, and two daughters—six of us altogether. Now how am I to share the goose equally, so that no one is offended?"

The peasant smiled craftily.

"Sire, permit me to divide it for you."

Taking a knife, he cut off the goose's head, saying, "Sire, you are the head of the household, thus you rightfully get the head."

Next he sliced off the goose's rump and handed it to the wife.

"Dear Lady, you sit at home all day looking after the house—so yours are the hindquarters."

Then he chopped off the feet and gave them to the sons.

"The feet are for you," he said, "because you are to follow in your father's footsteps."

And the daughters got the wings.

"Soon, my dear young ladies, you will fly from this house to find a husband—here are your wings."

"To be fair I'll take the rest for myself," he said, heading for the door.

The squire, greatly amused by the peasant's impudence, rewarded him with food—and money.

Now this story reached the ears of a rich peasant. Being envious, he quickly set to roasting five geese for the squire.

"I thank you for the geese," the squire said. "But, you see, I have a problem: Here are my wife, two sons, and two daughters—six altogether. How are we to share your five geese equally?"

The rich peasant was at a loss.

Thereupon, the squire sent for the poor peasant to ask his advice.

THE "DEAD" MAN AND THE BEAR

Two companions were on their way through a forest when they were suddenly attacked by a big brown bear. One quickly took to his heels, scrambled up a tree to safety, and hid, leaving the other behind.

What was the poor man to do? It was too late to flee.

Trembling with fear, he flung himself to the ground pretending to be dead. The bear was puzzled. He poked and sniffed the still form: first its toes and fingers, then its neck and hair.

The man was afraid to breathe.

After what seemed an age, the bear gave the fellow's ears a loud snuffle, grunted, and, thinking him really dead, ambled off through the trees.

No sooner was the bear out of sight than the first companion climbed down the tree, laughing with relief.

"Well, friend," he said, "what did that old bear whisper in your ear?"

The other smiled.

"He gave me some good advice," he said. "He told me to beware of those who leave their friends in danger . . ."

THE LITTLE BIRD

It was Misha's birthday and he had lots and lots of presents. But best of all was one from his uncle—a wooden bird cage. The cage was so cleverly made that it could catch birds all by itself: All you had to do was sprinkle seed upon a platform, hang the cage out of doors, let a bird fly in and perch on the platform. Then the platform would turn over, shutting the cage door at the same time.

Very simple.

Misha was overjoyed. He immediately ran to show the present to his mother. But she was not pleased at all.

"What a nasty contraption!" she exclaimed. "Why do you want to catch birds? Leave the poor things alone."

"I'll put them in my cage," explained Misha, "and they'll sing for me."

He found some seed, sprinkled it on the platform, hung the cage in the garden, and waited for birds to fly in.

But the birds were scared of him and would not come near.

After a while he went indoors to have his dinner and quite forgot about the cage. But when he had finished his meal and went into the garden, he was delighted to find a little bird fluttering inside the cage.

"Mama, look, I've caught a bird!" he shouted in his excitement. "It's a nightingale, I shouldn't wonder. See how fast its heart is beating."

But his mother said, "It's a sparrow. Now mind you don't harm it. Better let it go."

"No, no, I'll feed it and give it some water," cried Misha.

For two days Misha fed the little bird and cleaned out the cage. On the third day, however, he forgot about his sparrow and did not change its water or clean the cage.

His mother scolded him.

"Just as I said, you shouldn't put birds in cages. Better let it go."

"No, I won't forget again," said Misha. "I'll put some water in at once and clean the cage."

Misha opened the cage door, put in his hand and began to clean the cage floor. Meanwhile, the poor sparrow fluttered about the cage, beating its wings on the bars. When the cage was clean, Misha went for some water, forgetting to shut the door.

As soon as the little bird discovered the open door, it spread its wings and flew across the room to the window. But, not noticing the glass, it flew straight into the windowpane and dropped heavily upon the sill.

Hearing the strange noise, Misha ran back into the room and picked up the bird; though its heart was still beating, it now lay where Misha put it in the cage, on its breast, its wings outspread, breathing heavily.

Misha's eyes filled with tears as he gazed at his little bird.

"Mama, what am I to do?" he cried.

"There's nothing you can do, my son," replied his mother.

All through the day, Misha stayed by the cage, staring at the sparrow lying on its breast and panting fast.

When Misha went to bed the little sparrow was still alive.

For a long time he could not sleep. Each time he shut his eyes he saw his little sparrow lying on the floor of the cage. And in the morning, when he came downstairs, he found the bird upon its back, its tiny claws clenched tight, its body stiff and cold.

From that day on Misha never caught birds again.

THE PLUM STONE

Mother had bought a pound of plums, washed them, and left them on a big plate in the center of the table. They were for dinner.

Little Vanya had never tasted plums in all his life and was very curious. First he sniffed the fruit, wrinkled his nose at the pleasing smell, and decided he liked them very much. Dinnertime was still a long way off and Vanya could not wait.

As soon as he was alone in the dining room, he seized a big plum and ate it quickly.

When dinnertime came, Mother counted the plums and noticed that one was missing. She informed Father.

The whole family sat around the table to eat and, in the course of the meal, Father asked, "Now then, children, have any of you eaten a plum?"

Each child answered in turn: "No."

But Vanya turned as red as a lobster.

Then Father said, "It is wrong to steal a plum; but that's not all. You see, plums have stones and if you swallow a stone you'll die. That's what really bothers me."

This time Vanya went as pale as a sheet.

"No, no," he stuttered. "I threw the stone out of the window."

At that everyone laughed.

Poor Vanya burst into tears.

BETTER TO BE LEAN AND FREE THAN PLUMP AND CHAINED

A lean and hungry wolf came prowling by a village one frosty morning when he met a dog, sleek and well fed.

"Tell me, Cousin," said the wolf, "how is it you're so plump?"

"People feed me," said the dog.

"Is that so?" said the wolf in amazement. "And is your job hard in earning your keep?"

"Oh no," replied the dog. "All I do is guard the farmyard at night."

"And you get food for that?" asked the wolf. "If that's all there is to it, I'll join you. You've no idea how tough it is to find food in the wild."

"The Master is sure to feed you well," said the dog.

Eagerly licking his lips, the wolf set off with the dog to serve people. But just as the two animals were entering the yard, the wolf noticed a bald patch on the dog's neck.

"Hold on, Cousin," he exclaimed. "How did you come to lose your fur?"

"The chain rubbed it away. . . . You see, for most of the day and night I'm chained to a post."

"Then farewell to you, my poor Cousin," called the wolf as he ran off. "I've changed my mind about serving people after all. I may go hungry, but I prefer to be lean and free than plump and chained."

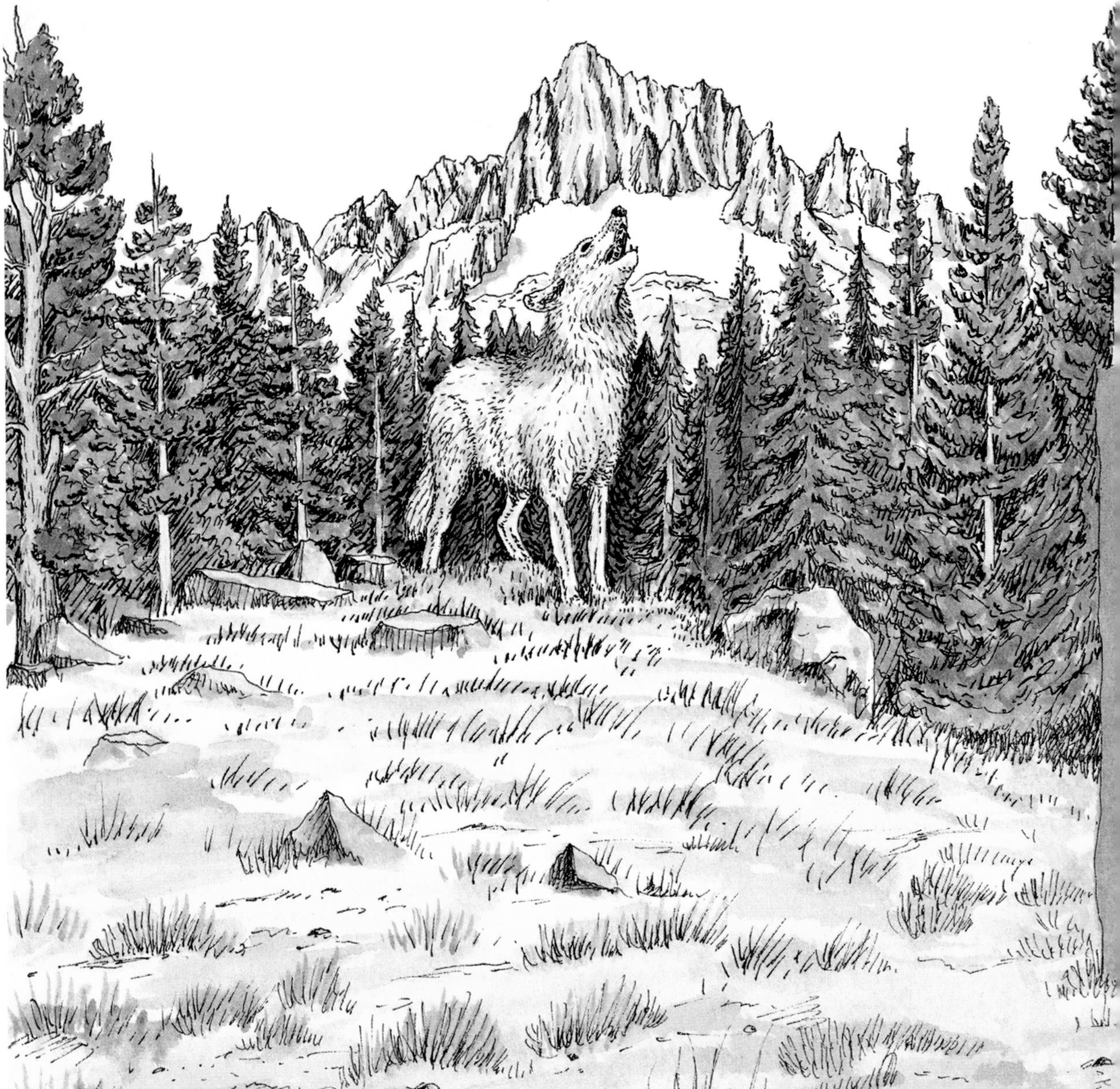

A YOUNG BOY'S STORY OF HOW HE DID NOT GO TO TOWN

Dad was going off to town.

"Dad, take me with you," I said.

But he shook his head.

"You'll freeze there. Stay home."

I turned around, burst into tears, and hid in the scullery. I cried and cried until I fell asleep.

In my dream I see a small path leading from our village to the chapel, and I see Dad walking along this path. So I catch up to him and off we go together to the city. As I go I see a chimney smoking ahead of us. So I say,

"Dad, is that the city?"

And he says,

"That's it."

Then we reach the chimney and I see them baking crusty rolls.

"Please, Dad, buy me a roll," I say.

So he does and gives it to me.

Then I woke up, put on my sandals and gloves and went outside. I could see my friends on the ice slides and sleds. I started to slide, too, and went on sliding until I was frozen stiff. I had only just got back home and climbed on top of the stove, when I heard Dad back from town. That cheered me up.

I jumped down and said, "Hello, Dad, did you buy me a crusty roll?"

"I did," he said, handing it over.

I hopped onto the bench and began to dance with joy.

DEW UPON THE GRASS

When upon a sunny summer's morning you go to the woods or fields, you may find diamonds among the grass. Those diamonds all sparkle and glitter in the sun with different colors—yellows and reds and blues. As you come nearer and take a closer look, however, you see it is really dewdrops caught in triangular blades of grass, glittering in the sunshine.

On the inside the blade of grass is as mossy and fluffy as velvet, and the droplets roll down it without leaving a wet mark.

If you're not careful in plucking a dewy blade, the droplet may cascade like a bright marble and disappear off the end of the stem before you notice it. Sometimes you can pick a tiny cup, put it slowly to your mouth, and drink the dew. That dew is sweeter than any drink in the world.

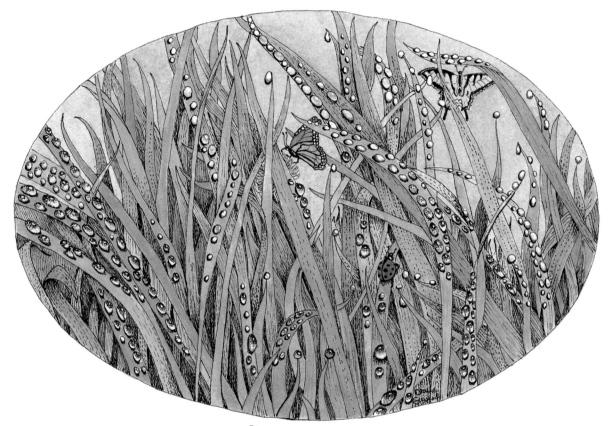

Clays Sievert

UNCLE JACOB'S DOG

Uncle Jacob was a watchman, that is to say he kept the village safe from wolves and bears. And he had a good helper in Old Bob—his shaggy dog with a white nose and large brown eyes.

Once, Uncle Jacob went into the forest for wood. Before leaving, he told his wife not to let the two children out of doors, for the previous night wolves had set upon and killed a neighbor's dog.

Yet no sooner was their father gone and their mother's back turned, than the children set to talking about the forest.

"I found a wild apple tree in a thicket yesterday," said the boy. "Its apples are so red and juicy. Let's go and pick some."

So they unlatched the door and slipped out unnoticed. Of course their poor mother was in despair when she found them missing. When Uncle Jacob came home he was very cross and hurried off into the forest in search of the children. He had not gone far when he heard the snarling of a wild animal and a soft whimpering. Quickly making for the spot, he soon arrived at an alarming scene.

There, huddled beneath a bush, were his two children, crying with fright. Uncle Jacob's faithful dog, who had protected them, was now being mauled savagely by a huge gray wolf. Without losing a moment, the old watchman took his axe and killed the wolf. Then he seized the children in his arms and quickly ran home before other wolves could attack.

The moment they were all safely inside the cottage, the door was bolted securely and the entire family sat down to supper. In his haste to save the children, however, the man had quite forgotten the brave old dog. And now, in the middle of the meal, there came a crying from behind the stout wooden door. Quickly unfastening the bolt, Uncle Jacob opened the door and there lay Old Bob, covered in blood and barely able to move.

Uncle Jacob brought him indoors and the children ran for some water and food, but the old fellow would take neither. He just licked their hands gratefully. Then, closing his tired brown eyes, he lay on his side and whimpered no more. The children thought he had fallen asleep. But, in truth, Old Bob was dead.

WHY WOLVES ARE MEAN AND SQUIRRELS FRISKY

A little red squirrel was skipping through the branches of a fir tree when—*plop!*—she fell right on the nose of a sleeping wolf.

In an instant the wolf was on his feet, fierce and bad-tempered, ready to eat the little pest who had disturbed him.

But the squirrel begged, "Please spare me, Wolf, I did not mean to wake you."

To tell the truth, the wolf had just had his dinner and was not very hungry.

"All right," he growled, "I'll spare you this time. But on one condition: You must tell me something I've always wanted to know. What makes you squirrels so frisky? As for me, I'm always mean and miserable. Yet whenever I look at you, I see you playing and skipping, as though you hadn't a care in the world."

"First let me go," replied the squirrel, "then I'll let you in on our secret."

The wolf let her slip from his paws and the squirrel scampered to safety up a tree. From there she called down:

"You're always so miserable because you're so mean; your meanness blackens your soul. We're always merry because we're kind and do nobody any harm."

THE ANTS

One day I went to the pantry for jam. As I picked up a jar from the floor I noticed it was covered with tiny black ants. They were everywhere: running down the sides of the jar, around the rim, and even in the jam itself.

Taking a spoon, I scooped out all the ants from the jam, brushed off the others from the jam jar, and placed it on the topmost shelf. Next day when I entered the pantry I noticed the ants had crawled up to the shelf and were again swarming around the jam jar.

This time I took down the jar, cleaned it once again, tied a string around the rim, and hung it from a hook in the ceiling. As I was leaving the pantry, I looked back at the jar and spotted one lone ant left on it: he was running fast around and around the jar.

I waited to see what would happen.

First the ant ran the length of the jar, seeming to examine all possibilities; then he ran along the string tied around the rim, up the string to the ceiling, and from the ceiling, he ran down the wall to the floor where a multitude of ants was waiting.

And do you know what? That clever ant must have told his friends how he had climbed down from the jar. . . . For in no time at all, an entire column of ants marched up the wall to the ceiling and along the string to the jar—taking exactly the same route as the first ant.

They're clever insects, aren't they?

FROM AN ACORN GREW AN OAK TREE TALL

One chill autumn morning, an old oak dropped an acorn. It rolled across the woodland path and came to rest beneath a hazel tree.

The hazel was most displeased.

"Don't you have space enough beneath your own branches?" it snapped. "Why don't you drop your acorns over there? I've hardly room for my saplings as it is!"

"I have lived these two hundred years," rumbled the old oak. "And the oakling that grows from my acorn will live just as long."

That made the hazel even angrier.

"And what if I smother your dear oakling? Then he won't last three days."

The oak did not reply. Silently he bade his son grow big and strong.

In the course of time, the acorn grew moist, burst its shell, and hooked one shoot into the soil, sending another climbing slenderly toward the sky.

Defiantly the hazel blocked out the sun. Yet the oakling struggled on bravely, seeming to grow even stronger in the shade.

A hundred years went by.

The hazel has long since withered and died. Yet from the tiny acorn an oak tree has grown tall and strong, proudly spreading its leafy mantle high above the forest.